Costa Rica

by Corey Anderson

Consultant: Marjorie Faulstich Orellana, PhD
Professor of Urban Schooling
University of California, Los Angeles

New York, New York

Credits

Cover, © Anatoliy Samara/Dreamstime and © SL_Photography/iStock; TOC, © Jose Michael Murillo Rojas/Getty Images; 4, © William Berry/Shutterstock; 5T, © Wollertz/Shutterstock; 5B, © Jorge A. Russell/Shutterstock; 7T, © Kryssia Campos/Getty Images; 7B, © florin1961/Getty Images; 8, © OGphoto/Getty Images; 9T, © Daniel Korzeniewski/Shutterstock; 9B, © Javier Fernández Sánchez/Getty Images; 10T, © Pedro Hélder da Costa Pinheiro/Getty Images; 10B, © Ondrej Prosicky/Shutterstock; 11, © Norbert Probst/Getty Images; 12, © SL_Photography/Getty Images; 13T, © Ferdy Timmerman/Shutterstock; 13B, © Eric Isselee/Shutterstock; 14, © hagit berkovich/Shutterstock; 15B, © The Art of Pics/Shutterstock; 15T, © Library of Congress/Wikimedia; 16T, © Gianfranco Vivi/Shutterstock; 16B, © Giuglio Gil/Hemis/ZUMA Press/Newscom; 17T, © Tati Nova photo Mexico/Shutterstock; 17B, © Robert Lessmann/Shutterstock; 18, © Ashok Charles/Getty Images; 19, © Steve bly/Alamy; 20B, © Kent Gilbert/Xinhua/Newscom; 20T, © patdu photography/Shutterstock; 21, © Cara Koch/Shutterstock; 22, © Jorge A. Russell/Shutterstock; 23, © OGphoto/Getty Images; 24, © apomares/Getty Images; 25T, © helovi/Getty Images; 25B, © Manueltrinidad/Getty Images; 26–27, © Jen Edney/Getty Images; 27, © Damocean/Getty Images; 28, © MB Photography/Getty Images; 29T, © THEPALMER/Getty Images; 29B, © THEPALMER/Getty Images; 30T, © Harry Hull III/Getty Images; 30B, © Anton_Ivanov/Shutterstock; 31(T to B), © Kryssia Campos/Getty Images, © johnbigdeal/Pixabay, © solucionindividual/Pixabay, © Free-Photos/Pixabay, © seanfboggs/Getty Images, and © Juan Carlos Vindas/Getty Images; 32, © Sergey Kohl/Shutterstock.

Publisher: Kenn Goin
Senior Editor: Joyce Tavolacci
Creative Director: Spencer Brinker
Design: Debrah Kaiser
Photo Researcher: Book Buddy Media

Library of Congress Cataloging-in-Publication Data

Names: Anderson, Corey, author.
Title: Costa Rica / by Corey Anderson.
Description: New York, New York: Bearport Publishing, 2020. | Series: Countries We Come From | Includes bibliographical references and index.
Identifiers: LCCN 2019014393 (print) | LCCN 2019015964 (ebook) | ISBN 9781642805840 (ebook) | ISBN 9781642805307 (library)
Subjects: LCSH: Costa Rica—Juvenile literature.
Classification: LCC F1543.2 (ebook) | LCC F1543.2 .A53 2020 (print) | DDC 972.86—dc23
LC record available at https://lccn.loc.gov/2019014393

Copyright © 2020 Bearport Publishing Company, Inc. All rights reserved. No part of this publication may be reproduced in whole or in part, stored in any retrieval system, or transmitted in any form or by any means, electronic, mechanical, photocopying, recording, or otherwise, without written permission from the publisher.

For more information, write to Bearport Publishing Company, Inc., 45 West 21st Street, Suite 3B, New York, New York 10010. Printed in the United States of America.

10 9 8 7 6 5 4 3 2 1

Contents

This Is Costa Rica 4

Fast Facts 30

Glossary 31

Index 32

Read More 32

Learn More Online 32

About the Author 32

This Is Costa Rica

Vibrant

Exciting

WILD

Costa Rica is a small country in Central America.

It lies between the Pacific Ocean and the Caribbean Sea.

Almost five million people live in Costa Rica.

Costa Ricans sometimes call themselves *Ticos* (TEE-kohs).

Costa Rica's land is incredible. The country has huge rain forests and sandy beaches.

Mountains and volcanoes cover much of Costa Rica.

There are over 60 volcanoes!

Arenal Volcano

crater

The Poás Volcano has a **crater** that's 1 mile (1.6 km) wide!

The country is filled with stunning animals.

Colorful parrots squawk in the trees.

Jaguars silently stalk **prey**.

Costa Rica's quetzal (ket-ZAHL) is a brightly colored bird. Its tail feathers can grow up to 3 feet (0.9 m) long!

Hawksbill sea turtles glide in the warm ocean waters.

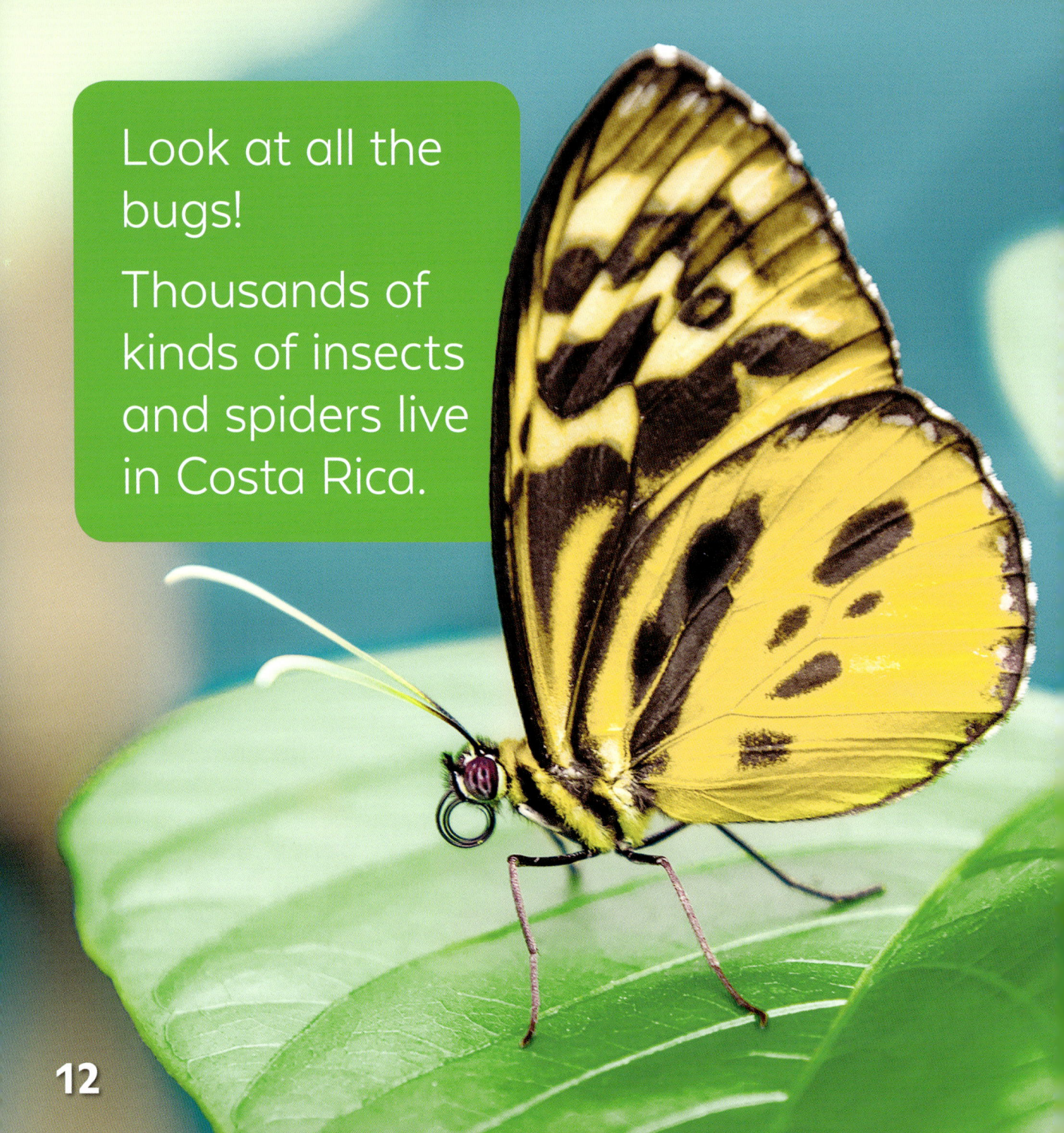

Look at all the bugs!

Thousands of kinds of insects and spiders live in Costa Rica.

The giant Hercules beetle is one of the world's strongest animals.

It can lift up to 100 times its own weight!

Hercules beetle

wandering spider

One of the deadliest spiders in the world is found in Costa Rica. It's called the wandering spider.

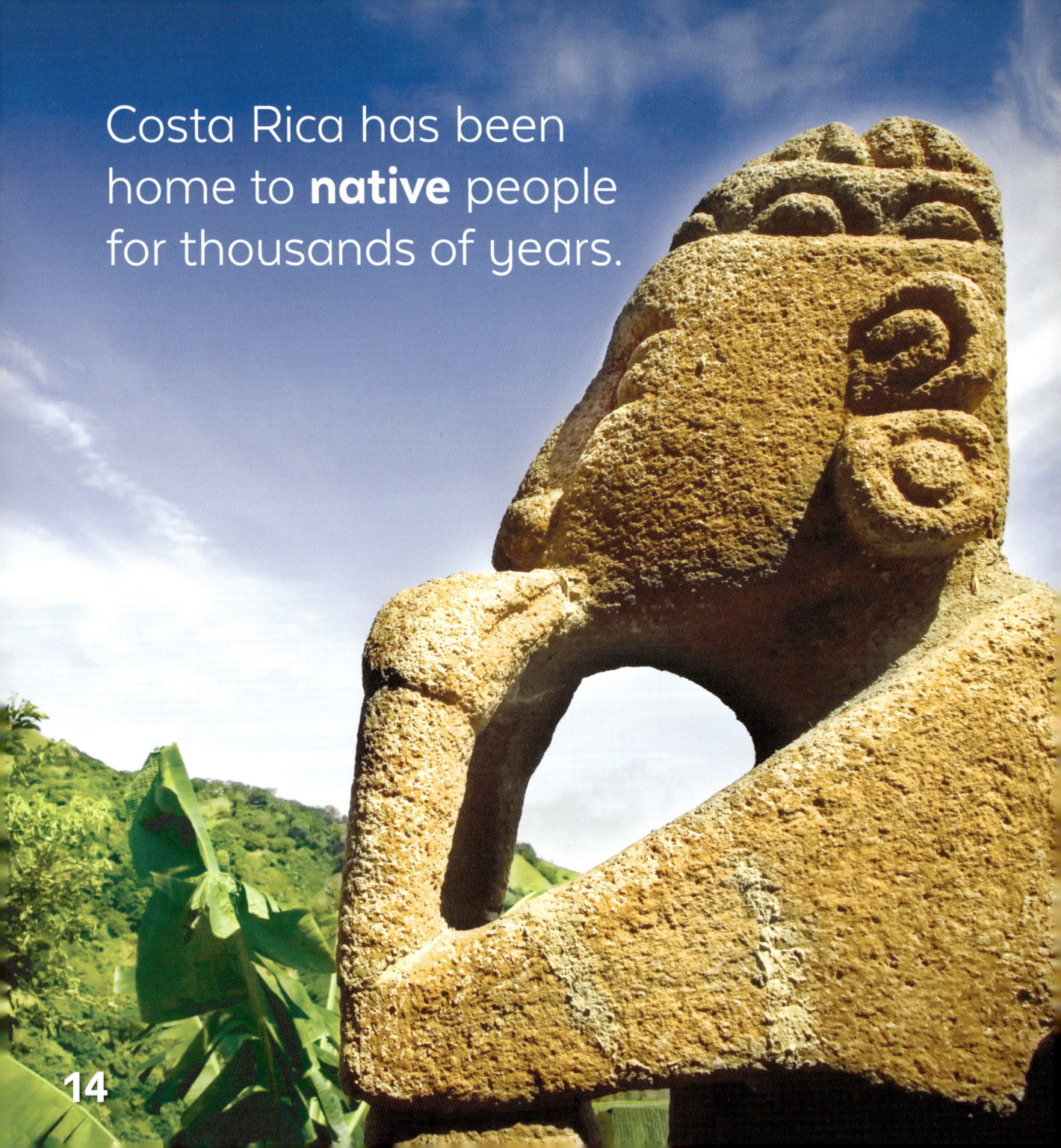

Costa Rica has been home to **native** people for thousands of years.

In the 1500s, the Spanish arrived, looking for gold.

They controlled the land for 250 years.

Costa Rica gained its **independence** from Spain in 1821.

San José (SAHN hoh-SAY) is Costa Rica's **capital** and largest city.

It rains almost half the year there!

Another city, Heredia, is called the City of Flowers. It has many beautiful gardens.

Coffee farms surround San José.

Costa Rican coffee is famous around the world!

coffee beans, also called cherries

Spanish is the main language of Costa Rica.

This is how you say *beach* in Spanish:

Playa (PLYE-uh)

This is how you say *dog*:

Perro (PEHR-oh)

Many native people in Costa Rica also speak their own languages.

It's time to celebrate!

Festival de la Luz, or the Festival of Light, is held in San José.

Fireworks light up the sky.

In December, a parade called El Tope Nacional is held in San José. It honors horses and riders!

Lively **floats** and dancers move down the city's streets.

Enjoying life is important in Costa Rica.

Many Costa Ricans live past 100 years of age.

Costa Ricans believe in *pura vida* (POO-ruh VEE-duh), which means "pure life" in Spanish.

The goal of pura vida is to live stress-free!

Costa Rican food is yummy! Tamales (tah-MAH-lez) are popular. They are made from corn and meat steamed in a banana leaf.

Gallo pinto (GUY-oh PEEN-toh) is rice, beans, and spices.

It's often served for breakfast.

Rice pudding is a delicious Costa Rican dessert.

Water sports are very popular in Costa Rica.

Surfers love to ride the country's big waves.

People also scuba dive and snorkel to see ocean wildlife.

Playa Jacó is a popular beach for surfers.

Nearly two million people visit Costa Rica each year! Many go hiking.

People also enjoy rafting and zip-lining. *Zoom!*

One zip line in Costa Rica stretches over 11 waterfalls!

Fast Facts

Capital city: San José

Population of Costa Rica: Almost five million

Main language: Spanish

Money: Costa Rican colón

Major religion: Catholic

Neighboring countries: Nicaragua and Panama

Cool Fact: There are over 10,000 different types of plants in Costa Rica!

Glossary

capital (KAP-uh-tuhl) the city where a country's government is based

crater (KRAY-tur) a large, round hole on the top of a volcano

floats (FLOHTS) moving platforms that carry displays in a parade

independence (in-duh-PEN-duhns) freedom from outside control

native (NAY-tiv) belonging to a particular place

prey (PRAY) an animal that's hunted and eaten by another animal

Index

animals 10–11, 12–13
capital 16–17, 20–21, 30
cities 16–17, 20–21, 30
food 17, 24–25

history 14–15
land 8–9
language 18–19, 30
lifestyle 22–23, 26–27

plants 16–17, 30
population 7, 30
religion 30
sports 26–27, 28–29

Read More

Raum, Elizabeth. *Costa Rica (Countries Around the World).* Chicago: Heinemann (2012).

Yomtov, Nel. *Costa Rica (Enchantment of the World).* New York: Children's Press (2014).

Learn More Online

To learn more about Costa Rica, visit
www.bearportpublishing.com/CountriesWeComeFrom

About the Author

Corey Anderson is a writer from Los Angeles who loves exploring destinations near and far with her husband, Josh, and sons, Leo and Dane.